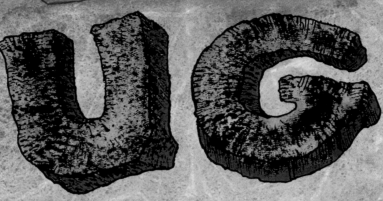

UG

BOY GENIUS OF THE STONE AGE AND HIS SEARCH FOR SOFT TROUSERS

RED FOX

For
TOM *"Why do they have trees?"* BENJAMIN,
CLARE, SARAH, CONNIE, MATILDA & MILES

A RED FOX BOOK: 0 09 941789 8

First published in Great Britain by Jonathan Cape,
an imprint of Random House Children's Books

Jonathan Cape edition published 2001
Red Fox edition published 2002

1 3 5 7 9 10 8 6 4 2

Red Fox Books are published by Random House Children's Books,
61-63 Uxbridge Road, London W5 5SA,
a division of The Random House Group Ltd,
in Australia by Random House Australia (Pty) Ltd,
20 Alfred Street, Milsons Point, Sydney, NSW 2061, Australia,
in New Zealand by Random House New Zealand Ltd,
18 Poland Road, Glenfield, Auckland 10, New Zealand,
and in South Africa by Random House (Pty) Ltd,
Endulini, 5A Jubilee Road, Parktown 2193, South Africa

THE RANDOM HOUSE GROUP Limited Reg. No. 954009
www.**kidsatrandomhouse**.co.uk

A CIP catalogue record for this book is available from the British Library.

Printed in Singapore by Tien Wah Press (PTE) Ltd

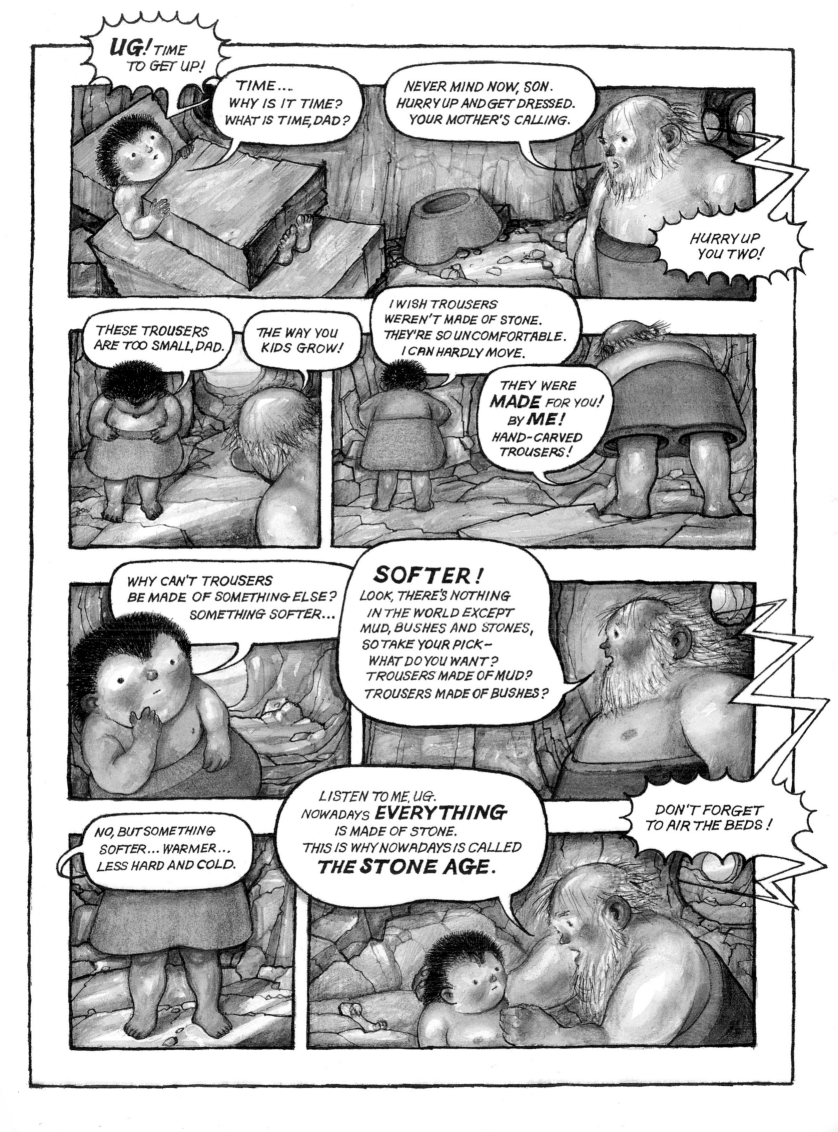

① WRITE: (anachronism) IN THE STONE AGE PEOPLE COULD NOT READ OR WRITE. THIS IS WHY DUG'S SPELLING IS SO POOR.

② IRON: (anachronism) IRON DID NOT EXIST IN THE STONE AGE. IRON WAS INVENTED IN THE IRON AGE WHICH CAME MUCH LATER: 4000000000000BC TO 20000000000 BC AND SO GAVE ITS NAME TO THE IRON AGE.

③ BUTTER: (anachronism) THERE WAS NO BUTTER IN THE STONE AGE. BUTTER IS COW'S MILK GONE SOLID AND TAME COWS DID NOT YET EXIST. THEY WERE STILL RUNNING WILD WITH THE PRE-HISTORIC MONSTER BULLS AND SO NO ONE COULD MILK THEM AND MAKE IT INTO BUTTER.

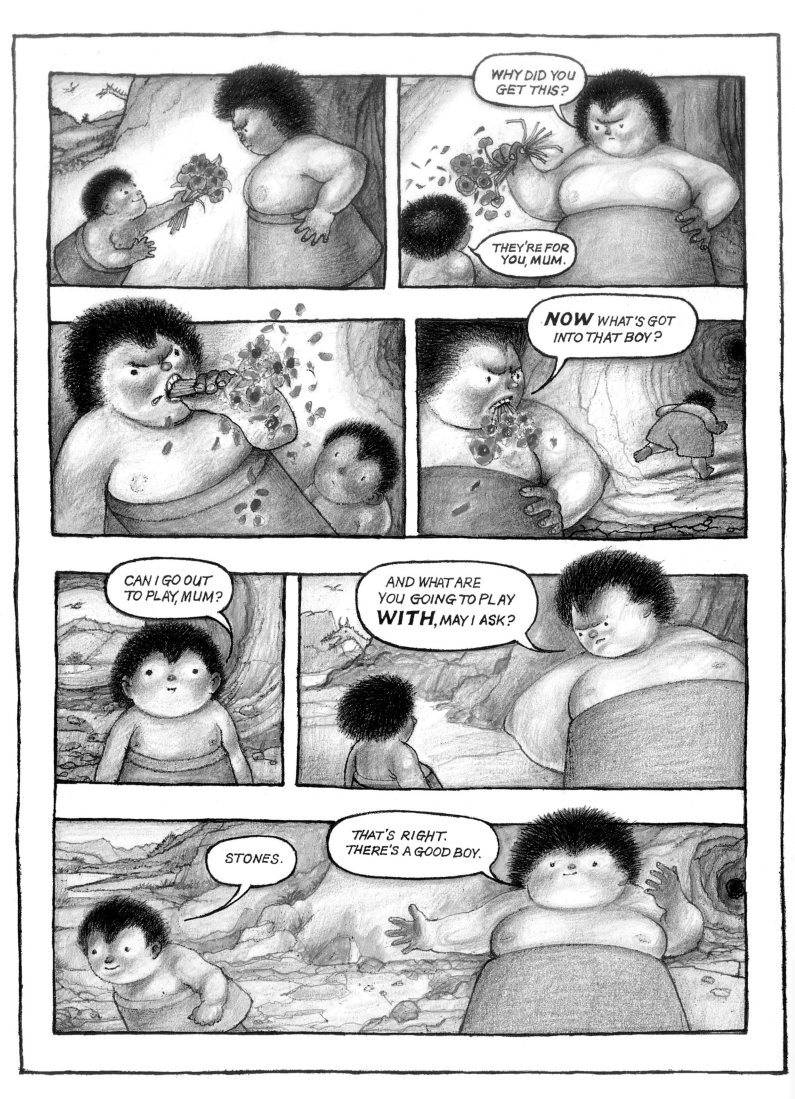

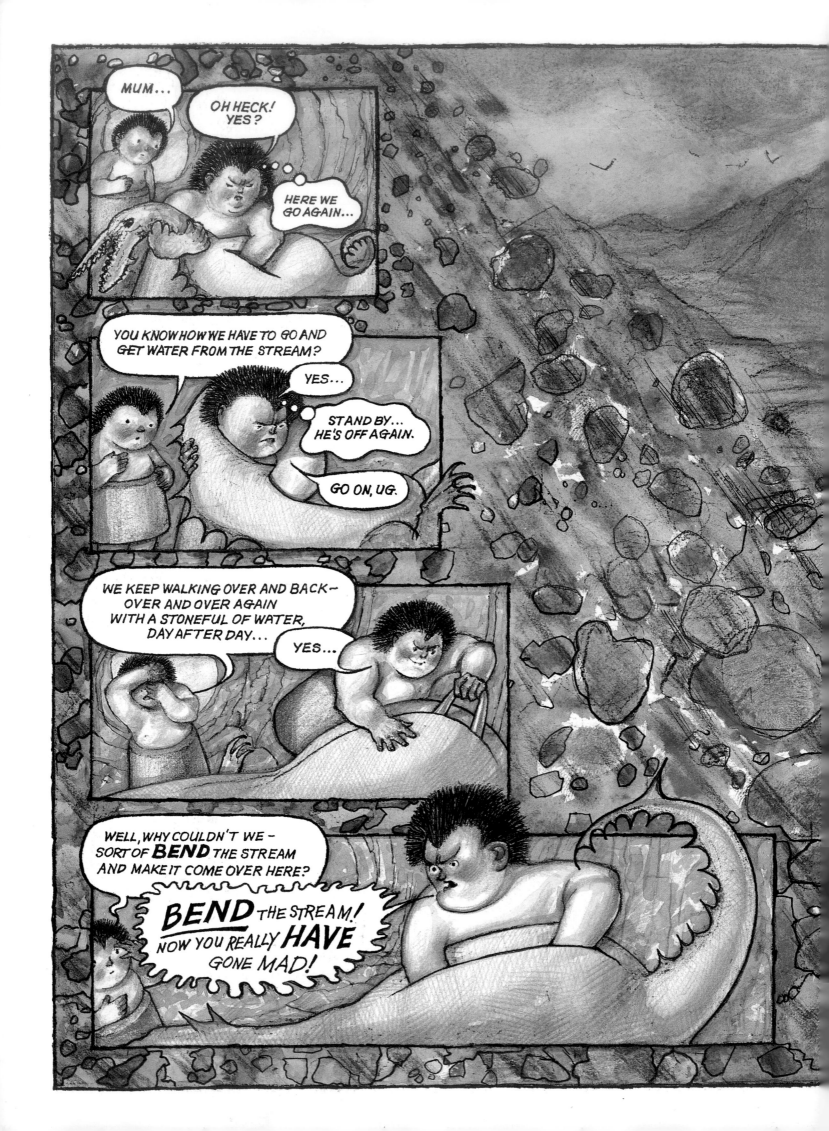

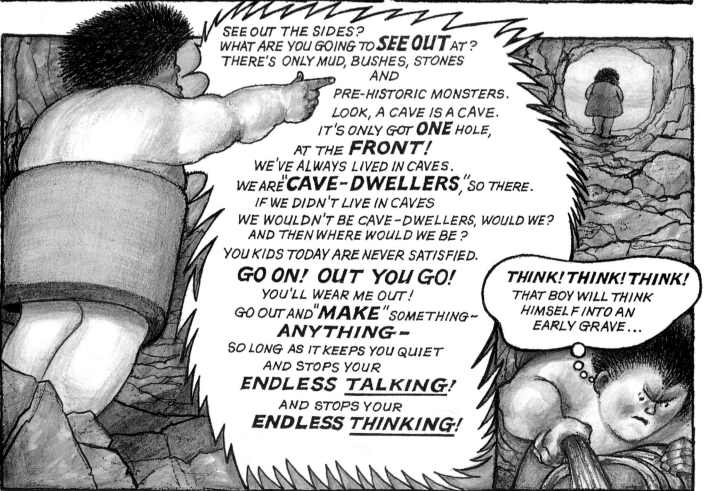

① WEEK: (anachronism)
THERE WERE NO "WEEKS" IN THE STONE AGE,
NOR WERE THERE "MONTHS" OR "YEARS."
IN THE STONE AGE, TIME STOOD STILL.
THIS IS WHY SO LITTLE PROGRESS WAS MADE
AND WHY IT TOOK AN AGE TO COME TO AN END.

② LUNCH: (possible anachronism)
IT IS NOT KNOWN FOR CERTAIN
WHAT THE MIDDAY MEAL WAS
CALLED IN THE STONE AGE.

③ SISYPHUS: (anachronism)
SISYPHUS CAME MUCH LATER,
AFTER HISTORY STARTED.
HE WAS A GREEK (OR A ROMAN)
AGES AGO (POSSIBLY EVEN BC).
HE PUSHED STONES UPHILL,
LET THEM ROLL DOWN AGAIN,
THEN PUSHED THEM UP AGAIN,
LET THEM ROLL DOWN, PUSHED
THEM UP AGAIN, LET THEM
ROLL DOWN, THEN PUSHED THEM
UP AGAIN. HE KEPT ON DOING
IT FOR YEARS, OVER AND OVER
AGAIN, FOR YEARS AND YEARS.
HE BECAME FAMOUS FOR DOING IT.

② SUMMER HOLIDAY: (anachronism)
SUMMER HOLIDAYS WERE UNKNOWN
IN THE STONE AGE.
ALTHOUGH NO ONE WENT TO WORK,
THE STRUGGLE FOR SURVIVAL WAS SO HARD,
DUE TO THE STONY CONDITIONS, THE MUD
AND THE ENORMOUS NUMBER OF BUSHES
THAT THERE WAS LITTLE TIME LEFT
FOR HOLIDAYS. SO THEY WERE UNKNOWN.
   FURTHERMORE, THE CLIMATE WAS
COMPLETELY DIFFERENT TO THE PRESENT
DAY AND "SUMMER" WAS PROBABLY
UNKNOWN DUE TO THE CLIMATE
BEING COMPLETELY DIFFERENT.

③ BOOTS: (anachronism)
BOOTS WERE ALMOST UNKNOWN IN THE
STONE AGE. ANIMALS WITH LEATHERY
SKINS HAD NOT YET EVOLVED, AS ALL
THE ANIMALS WERE STILL PRE-HISTORIC
MONSTERS. SUCH BOOTS AS DID EXIST
WERE MADE OF STONE AND WERE
ALMOST AS UNCOMFORTABLE AS THE
STONE TROUSERS. SO THEY WERE NEVER
USED. CONSEQUENTLY, NO STONE AGE
BOOT HAS EVER BEEN FOUND, AND
OF COURSE, NEVER A PAIR.